T0193927

Teacher TURNED GANGSTA

Juven Bailey

authorHOUSE®

AuthorHouse™ UK
1663 Liberty Drive
Bloomington, IN 47403 USA
www.authorhouse.co.uk
Phone: 0800 047 8203 (Domestic TFN)
*   +44 1908 723714 (International)*

Published by AuthorHouse 05/22/2019

ISBN: 978-1-5462-9892-2 (sc)
ISBN: 978-1-5462-9893-9 (e)

Contents

Chapter 1

Theirs was a post-war industrial building. Their school that is. Converted and extended into finery by adding new teaching huts every few years; with their own imaginative take on central heating. They overlook a park and a wasteland, a few streets down from the high road. They are very kind to immigrants and their population keeps increasing as they offer excellent EAL (English as an additional language) learning. Heathrow and Gatwick love them, children enter, and they receive. It helps the books. They are happy there; all the Ofsted (Office of Standards in Education, Children Services and Skills) surveys say so.

The corridors are narrow and painted a garish yellow, with pictures oozing nostalgia, from the visit of the Queen, to the manager of a popular football club in the 1980's and the visit of the Beatles. They love their memories, the good old days and so on and so forth.

The main building is a square with two teaching huts in the side gap. There are two further brick made buildings to the back, near the park, by the drains, by the children's play area, where the raw sewage runs. The children don't mind. They are used to things stinking in their school.

To the left of the brown-coloured, out-house-like building is the garden, a vision of the ECO (eco-friendly) team. There are flowers and vegetables which you can still recognise between the weeds. Mrs. Russell, in charge of the ECO team, has been off sick, very sick, sick and tired.

To the left of the science block, is part of the school wall. Plans are afoot to add barbed wire to the top, to prevent our more creative students from climbing over and escaping. But there is a crack in the wall. Large enough for contraband: chips, burgers, chewing gum, fizzy drinks, all the goods the new healthy eating menu in the canteen doesn't permit; all the things that satisfy the soul; and desperate sixth formers are only too happy to supply. You see, they are allowed out at lunch, to a temporary oasis. The rest just smell and dream about beyond the fences.

To the front of the square are some of the offices of the important people: the two deputy heads, the bursar, site manager and the great "Him". Yes, the great "him", "him" who deemed it necessary to gently encourage staff to retire early or take a redundancy package, and then replaces them with shiny new NQTs (Newly Qualified Teachers), pretty pennies, ready to spend. He's particularly fond of little Gemma *'the bubbling enthusiasm of the future'* as he describes her. He often shows her the grounds, particularly the area near to the wasteland through the path where they come from. Perhaps she could be the next ECO teacher if Russell doesn't come back. In their animated conversation, his passion for new and exciting ventures is strong. Gemma has a first degree from the IOE (Institute of Education), he likes that.

God knows he had seen too much incompetence in the last round of lesson observations. Old methods, not enough use of technology, rigid thinking within the box, children nearly comatose. *God, he mused, when will we bring back real learning, something relevant to this generation, something out there, something ground-breaking.* These thoughts tumble over each other as he makes his way to the canteen to eat his lunch with great demonstration, with gusto. The school must be convinced he has made the right choice when selecting the new caterers. As he bites into his risotto, which he notes has a distinctive cheesy smell, the last thought wins. *How do you get a teacher from a grade three to a grade one?* The sound of his fork hitting his metal tray reverberates around the room.

There is silence. The white noise seems endless, but the canteen soon resumes its usual flurry of activity. A few moments later he spots Brenda and resumes to chew a bit faster, she would surely join him, he would bet his hat on it and he was not in a mood for discussing what action should be taken since John and Brian were kicked out of the PRU (Pupil Referral Unit). The two wankers! Brenda is nice enough, but not a woman of the future. She still thinks everybody can be reformed, plus she is partial to pickled onions, something which lingers on the breath. A quick exit was necessary.

As he shovels in a few forkfuls, etiquette forgotten, he sees Brenda looming through the corner of his left eye, and the only excuse he can think of pops into his head. The loo, he must make a desperate rush for the loo.

'Hello George.'

Yes, that's what "the him" is called. George Nobbs.

'Hi Brenda, come join me'. 'How are things going?'

'As good as can be, I've had a busy morning phoning parents ... ahh these children, when you realise the kind of parents they have, you see some of them just need a little bit of love.'

'Yes, yes, quite so. We must do all we can. You must try the risotto, it's quite good.' He gestures toward the staff lunch queue.

Brenda doesn't budge.

'I am quite impressed with the new caterers'

he maintained, 'I like that they have a fresh fruit selection with all meals.'

Brenda half raises from her seat to get some view of the serving trays and then sits back down.

Still no success.

'Have you heard what our John and Brian have gotten themselves into?'

Oh shit! Literally. It was just the line of conversation he had hoped to avoid; he had a curriculum meeting in half an hour and the woman from the borough was coming at three. It wasn't a good time to discuss John and Brian's theft from the PRU; after all, the police were already dealing with it. That nice PCSO (Police Community Support Officer) seemed capable enough to handle the situation, for now, it's best to let the law take its course.

'Yes, yes this time they must be dealt with harshly, but I'm afraid I have to rush Brenda. I've got a pressing matter that must be dealt with', he said gesturing towards the toilets, 'which good breeding and manners prevents me from detailing.'

Brenda's shoulders hunched allowing her ample bosom to bubble forward and peek over her Bonmarché striped top. Her cheeks take on a rosier glow as she watches him take his exit.

Chapter 2

To the rear of the school, behind the library is an office. It is sparsely decorated with off-white walls and two rectangular windows which seem like eyes in an owl's head. At the front of the room, there is a wooden desk and a blue office chair where the padding is peeling showing a discoloured brown sponge. To the left is a noticeboard with a few poems and attendance and attainment certificates held by a red thumb tack. There is also a picture of Beyoncé with the title of one of her tracks "Sugar Mama".

The carpet is threadbare and, in the corner, near to the grey filing cabinet, you can see the floor. Two faint footprints are also visible on the wall, adjacent to each other on either side of the blue chair.

In this office sits a bird. A human one. Charlotte deputy head of year 9, is nearly six feet tall and as thin as a rail.

Her hair is cropped short and a mousy brown. On either side of her thin bony nose are deep set, shifty blue eyes. She is a woman with no visible curves and is rather fond of Primark's pencil skirts. Today, she has complemented a mustard skirt with a fitted pinstriped white and blue shirt and cream mules. She is perched on the edge of the desk in deep thought.

Charlotte is a born fighter, daughter of an Irish butcher and a hairdressing mother, full of grit and fight. She is the first in three generations since they moved to England to have gone to university, the family is very proud of her.

She hasn't had a bath in three days.

Charlotte isn't one to waste time, she knows she has a year team review on Friday with management and she is determined to make an impression. Hygiene can be overlooked for more important matters like studying the year group data, analysing the statistics, comparing it to other year groups in the borough, seeing the trends in outstanding local schools and seeing how her school compares. She knows they are not too happy with the current head of year and this is her shot to upstage, show them who should really be in charge. She is fond of Kim, but she is fonder of success. She had seen Kim's notes for the meeting that had fallen out of her folder and she had already read them before she returned it to her, they were unimpressive. She had also secretly recorded some of their conversations where Kim had vented her venomous hatred for the new headteacher, just as an insurance policy, just in case she ever needed it. She had also embedded the best of Kim's ideas into her presentation. Nobody could accuse her of elbowing her way to the top-everybody was doing it! It's the nature of the game.

During the last week, she had deliberately loitered around the staff toilet area to come upon the head a few times, to strike up that necessary casual conversation. He seemed pleasant enough with her and that was a good sign. All the chips were in place, silently waiting for the game to begin. She didn't want to focus on her personal problems, forget the fact she thought she might be pregnant. That could never be allowed to manifest. Everybody knows in this career, as a woman, that one ill-timed breeding, having that one child is the difference between being head or deputy head. A lot goes on while you are on maternity leave, a hell of a lot, and when the baby comes along nobody says it, but it's as if you have a disability that prevents you from functioning, prevents you from being a professional. You are even looked at with specks of pity as if you have arrived to work with the baby swinging loosely from your chest only attached by a nipple.

She wondered what she should wear for this meeting. One of the deputy heads was strictly religious so that rules out her sheer Marks and Spencer navy blue top-she mustn't show any flesh. Something would come up though, that was the least of her worries. This meeting was big and being prepared was the key. Her note to self was "do not mispronounce pedagogy". She always did.

Despite being a game player, Charlotte cared for her students and often spent time working with them hours after school-even when managers weren't looking. She knew the value of education, it had now begun to make a difference in her family. She would never forget the look on her gran's face when she graduated from Brunel with first class honours, nor the tears of joy that trickled through the wrinkles on her tiny face as she uttered,

'*You ain't never cleaning the floor like me love*', triggering Charlotte's own tears.

Nevertheless, forget the sentiments, the pregnancy scare, the infected tattoo she got from the parlour in Vegas during half-term. The meeting was fast approaching, and she had to be ready.

Chapter 3

In a ground floor flat in a not so nice part of North London, Mary turns the key in her door and comes home to a shell of a man. Her man. Her husband. His eyes are glazed over, and he smiles as she approaches. He's got a Bible in his left hand and a can of Foster's beer just by his right hand beside the couch on which he is sat. His eyes dart wildly all over her body and he reclines further with a sigh of resignation as she enters. He seems content. Mary looks at him, takes note of the green joggers, red top and Homer Simpson socks she gifted him last Christmas. The sound of her heart breaking is almost audible; remorse, fear, anger and loneliness creeps into the room and hugs her until it becomes a death grip, a strangling hold which chokes words out of her lips.

'Hi,' she chirps with feigned enthusiasm.

'Bless the Lord, oh my soul and all that is within me (and you) bless his holy name' Adebola responds with fervour 'And how are you, o?'

'I would say I am good, but I would be lying, I had my tenth failed lesson observation today.'

'The devil is a liar, rebuke the devil and he will flee from you.'

'Well if only he would flee. He hasn't, and he is waiting for me at work tomorrow with an action plan.'

'Call upon the Lord in time of trouble, the Bible tells us He is a present help.'

'Yes, but could you help me now? "The garbage needs putting out surely you don't need the Lord for that?'

The putrid smell of waste mixed with lager had greeted her the minute she entered the door. And so, it continues...

Mary had migrated from Nigeria. A decision she had always questioned. She was the daughter of Chief Wale Otunba and had moved to the United Kingdom in 2001 a trained and qualified teacher in her country, but that meant nothing in the UK. She was a proud woman whose father was a chief in the village, an owner of land and assets, three wives and twenty children. She was the daughter of the senior wife. She had always enjoyed the prestige of being royalty; having house help and servants, she was the daughter of a chief. Nobody had prepared her for the emotional turbulence of establishing a career in the United Kingdom-something she had seen destroy her husband. He was a teacher by profession too, but who could tell? Who would link the pathetic lump, the useless man on the sofa to be a trained professional? At times she thinks she should never have married Adebola against her father's wishes.

He had wanted someone of better status for his princess. Thank God she was only a partial fool; Adebola had wanted her pushing out children left right and centre. Mary took triple birth control. Maybe she should never have become a teacher.

When she had expressed an interest in having a career it was naturally assumed she would go into something more gentle-perhaps event planning, bridal fashion retail or even jewellery making. But no. In her bid to save the world, she had chosen to teach, a final wound in the relationship between her and her father.

She reminisces over the uphill climb to establish herself and the mostly emotional pitfalls. She had been highly rated in her Nigerian school. It was, to say the least, a bitter blow, a heartrending shock, a metaphoric whiplash to discover that she was grossly under qualified according to British standards. Did they not design, spearhead the creation of the education system in her country? So, when the hell did it become so substandard?

Anyway, after finding out the requirements she needed for teaching in London, she was more than a little pleased to get a job offer through an agency. For her, it was the beginning of bright new things. A brilliant new life in the first world, far more politically stable (Her grandparents had suffered under Abacha the dictator, who ruled ruthlessly in the time of a broken Nigeria, now there was religious unrest) Here there are much better-resourced schools than she had ever experienced, and all the children speak and write perfect English. Right? Surely, because after all, this was the country in which the language was born.

Talk about a skewed perspective! It didn't take her long before a letter from NARIC (National Academic Recognition Information Centre) showed how bottom of the barrel she was, whose teaching qualifications were equivalent to just A "Level" study! This had sent her into depression for weeks, nights of crying, outright wailing into the early hours of the morning until she subsided into bouts of shaking or seized into fitful sleep. Mary was hurt. It was not only the sense of being undervalued, but her pride was hurt. She is a chief's daughter!

After a month of an almost malignant self-pity, crazed rage, absolute desolation, Mary had a moment of clarity, the old adage:" When in Rome do as the Romans" It was then she began the long painful process of becoming a qualified teacher, conversely, it was then, her husband who had received the same news, curled up and died. Well, he's not dead, not really, the bastard is sitting on the sofa, but he's as good as.

She had done the first degree, thank God for the OU (Open University) and she had obtained the Holy Grail, QTS (Qualified Teachers Status). Now this! Lesson observation after observation deemed mostly unsatisfactory or a damn grade 3. Now Sharon from the borough, a mere girl, was coming to mentor her! She didn't even have much life or teaching experience, but she was coming to mentor her-the bloody cheek as they say. It didn't help that in staff training half the time they mentioned things she had already done in her country. For example, Bloom's Taxonomy. Hasn't anyone had a bloody thought since Benjamin Bloom? Knowledge, Comprehension, Application, Analysis, Synthesis and Evaluation. For shit sake, she could say it in her sleep! Questioning, the art of questioning, well Mary had a question she needed answering. How is it that after each lesson observation the oral feedback was so positive, so buoyant, yet the written feedback was nothing short of shit? A question. Synthesise, analyse, evaluate, whatever. Just answer that!

Chapter 4

The young man coming down the corridor is Sean. He is wearing a suit two sizes too big and oversized black-rimmed glasses that make his eyes seem huge and wide, he's cute and he knows it. He drives a Skoda and is the child of an English mother from Bethnal Green and a Jamaican father who hails from Tottenham. He sees himself as a product of his mother depleting Anglo-Saxon stock and often resented his mixed-race heritage despite liking the current marketability of it, and the increased popularity of his now commercial look. He's a man who lives on the planet of mixed emotions and sometimes there is pain sewn into his veins. He thinks his mixed heritage excludes him from things or is it only in his head? Sean had his own philosophy regarding teaching and his view was affixed. As far as he was concerned it was more important to be liked than competent. Being loved was ninety percent of the battle.

As he approaches the staff room he sees, through the glass door, members of the science faculty huddled together, he decides to join them, after all he is a man of all faculties. It doesn't take long for his mood to sour.

'... Yes, that's the best investment right now; banks aren't giving any decent interest rates, might as well put your money there.'

'Another thing you could try is...' The conversation tapers off as they see him approach.

'Don't stop on my account...keep the conversation flowing', Sean pipes up.

'Sean my man, wat's up yo? You finished those progress reports?'

That was Howard. One summer camp in America and he was convinced he was American, accent and all.

'There's still time, I'm going to see Kath anyway because it's not feasible to get them done in such a tight time frame. By the way, what was that about investments?'

'That's boring talk man, did you do anything sweet over the hawlidaay?' he drawled.

'No nothing different just hanging out with the missus.' Sean spat.

'So, you're not divulging any of the banking secrets? Spill the beans.'

'Sean man, ain't nothing but a chicken wing-chill out. We got time to talk money. I wanna hear what's going on with you and your Boo.'

It's a good thing Howard was mostly oblivious to things around him. He didn't even notice Sean's complexion going darker, the new stiffness in his neck and the beginning of a twitch, like the Incredible Hulk Sean was beginning a metamorphosis, but before he could retort the shrill of the fire alarm jolts everyone into action. It was the third time this week, you could bet there wasn't a real fire, that little twat John probably set it off again. He and his cousin were taking turns. If only parents knew what teachers had to do on a day to day basis! They would probably sew up their wombs.

This fire alarm is a saviour because Sean was too tempted to slap Howard. He needed to walk, to subdue this anger that was pumping in his veins.

Howard wouldn't tell him, wouldn't bloody tell him about the investment idea, and he knew why. It was always the same; because he was a mixed-race kid with an English mother and a black father from Tottenham.

Chapter 5

George Nobbs is running. This for most is a singular experience. How often do you see a headteacher running? From behind it is worth filming. In his grey trousers his cheeks do not operate in unison. The left cheek is spasmy and jiggles frantically almost as if it would spill unceremoniously onto his hipbone. The right cheek is strangely firm and holds on like dough that has set. It's almost as if he is wearing Spanx on one half of his body. Unusual, very unusual.

Behind him is little Gemma, they have been working long and hard, he's really into her. What a brilliant mind. He was blown by her prodigious ideas. She wasn't in a full sprint but is clearly flustered and in a half run; nothing like George's Usain Bolt performance though. The reason for this little exhibition? Ofsted is coming.

George was not an ungrateful man. He thanked God for his job. He had been a deputy head for five years and had been looking for progression for a while. When this job was advertised (the previous head had been found dead, in his closet, wearing a red and black PVC dominatrix outfit) that last bit wasn't mentioned in the local news, this had been his chance for progression. He fought off five other candidates for the job and when he was appointed it was a cause for celebration among his friends, family and the assistant heads in his old school who had been praying for him to die. You see, they were looking for progression too. George wasn't lazy, he knew being a head teacher was no ride in the park, he was up for the challenge, but by God, some days it was like giving birth through the ass.

The reputation of his school was notorious, and he knew Ofsted was due, he just didn't expect them so quickly. Too much had gone on in the prior regime-the word had not yet been invented in the English language to describe the last school report. Disastrous, catastrophic, calamitous even ruinous did not come close. He knew at least some kind of monitoring visit was due, but he had hoped he would have had more time to implement changes. So far, he had done his best to get rid of the old fogies who were like dead weight on the school. It sounds unkind but some of them were to the school what the iceberg was to the Titanic. He had done two stringent rounds of lesson observations and was very aware of his Achilles heels, enough for ten pairs of feet, one of whom, by the way, was his co-observer; but nevertheless, he was determined to plod on. He had spoken to the borough about a mentoring programme and already, with the help of Gemma and other working party members, drafted an internal programme. He had got human resources to tidy up all teachers' files making sure DBS's (Disclosure and Barring Services) reports were up to date and there were no criminals on the lurk. The canteen menu had been revised, more in line with the healthy eating agenda; the front of the school had been painted; a redraft of the extracurricular offerings was done, starting next term the girls would have gymnastics and the boys would be partaking of fencing and ceramics.

Now here he was, doing what he hadn't done since high school. Running. This ill-fated visit would make anyone act uncharacteristically, he must put the army on high alert, he must erect the defence barricades, he must plan for the one lesson he taught each fortnight, but most importantly, he must stop Bentley, his deputy head, from sending that letter to the governors.

As he rounds the corner, he sees Charlotte ahead near the men's toilet. Funny, why did that seem like déjà vu? Anyway, no time to speak, no time for pleasantries, he must get to his office and ring the alarm.

Chapter 6

Charlotte is fuming, she is absolutely pissed! Ofsted is coming, and the timing couldn't be worse. The meeting she had been planning for, waited for with bated breath was postponed. She couldn't have been more prepared if she had tried. She knew the year group as if they were her own children, better than Kim ever would. She knew all the data, the at-risk children, the year group's attainment on its own, the year group's attainment in comparison to the school down the road, the data in comparison to the whole borough, even how the data compared nationally. She was ready. Her outfit had been carefully chosen, she was going to wear a suit, all black-no sheer, nobody would be offended. Her PowerPoint was prepared; one of the IT guys had added the final touches. Her files were impeccable, she had spoken to George on a social level as often as she could, mostly by the toilets, except for earlier when he blasted past her in such a rush without even a mere acknowledgement. That was excusable though, Ofsted was coming.

She had often mused at the power of Ofsted and knew that after she was tired of being a head teacher she would become an Ofsted inspector. Imagine the power? You walk into a school for two and a half days and you get to determine the immediate future of hundreds-staff and students. A damning report can cause a huge fall in intake, the need for redundancies, loss of jobs, morale damage and depleted self-worth. Major reforms are made to the point where a school becomes unrecognisable, a place where people who once worked in unison and relative peace became a warzone where once loving people, recognisably human, were now backstabbing ghouls with open mouths dribbling diatribe. Not to mention the local community; once the report hit the internet or was roughly edited by a local reporter for the ever so receptive local news; being associated with the school was equivalent to instigating an outbreak of Ebola.

Anyway, back to the matter at hand. The damned meeting was postponed.

Before Charlotte could think hard about how to use the delay to her advantage, she was ripped from her momentary contemplation by an urgent rattle on the office door. She opened the door to a most unexpected visitor. Sean Williams.

This was more than a surprise, why was he there? Perhaps to see Kim. Charlotte hardly spoke to Sean, yes, she saw him around and yes, she had invited him to one of her house parties but in the end, she had assessed him as an annoying liability. He is cute and she had once complimented him on his ass, she had even maintained the fantasy of a roll in the sack with him for about a week and then dismissed it. He would be no good for her career, Sean had a reputation as a lazy, incompetent brown nose and there was no way she could be associated with that kind. Your friends were makers or breakers of your career. What the hell did he want?

'Hi Charlotte.'

'Hey Sean.' What brings you to these parts? Kim's out for the afternoon.' Charlotte quickly adds.

'Oh is she?' he responds swiftly scanning the surroundings and settling himself down on a nearby chair.

'Actually, Charlotte I am here to see you, by the way I hope you don't mind me saying, but that mustard looks great on you, that's not a colour every woman could pull off.'

Charlotte nearly farted. Anything to get rid of him and his nonsense. It was clear he wanted something and with lessons to plan for tomorrow, she didn't want to prolong the guessing game.

Through a strained smile, she answered

'Thanks Sean, how can I help you?'

'You are an incredible deputy head of year and I need your advice; I'm hoping you could take me under your wings.'

It was nothing but an act of divine intervention that Charlotte was able to suppress a scoff.

'Sean you flatter, but how exactly can I be of help?'

'Well some might think this a bit premature, but I am thinking of applying for the deputy head of year post being advertised and as you have made that transition I was wondering if you could give me some advice for success.'

Charlotte was convinced this was a sick joke-too damn sick to laugh. The chance of Sean being DHOY (Deputy

Head of Year) was equivalent to hell freezing over twice. She hoped her thoughts weren't imprinted on her face.

'...well we have to be ambitious, haven't we?' I tell you what Sean I'm pressed for time. Can we follow through on this some other time? Do you know Ofsted's in tomorrow?

'Yes, yes they'll come, and they'll go.' He countered unperturbed.

Mentally Charlotte kicked him in the nuts.

'Well I have a full teaching day tomorrow, I have lesson plans to do, Power Points to improve and I must review some data for the year group just in case the inspectors want to interview me.'

'Thanks for your time Charls we'll catch up soon after this circus is over.' Sean threw over his shoulder as he headed for the door.

At the door, he reaches for the handle and then hesitates. Sean bends over and his jacket lifts ever so slowly, seductively, exposing his rear, he needlessly adjusts his shoelaces and twerks, yes twerks, before unfolding upright and slithering through the door.

On his exit, Charlotte changes gear into robot mode. The computer is switched on and she waits for it to boot up, her mobile is taken off silent and the recent hard copies of the year group data are ripped from the drawer. She immediately clicks on the email icon to check recent correspondence. She had twenty emails since lunchtime.

- *Ofsted's in tomorrow*
- *No detentions this afternoon*
- *School will open till midnight tonight*

- *The HOYS, DHOYS and HODS were needed for a cuddle at four o clock.*
- *Think of ways to hide John and Brian -pay them not to come in tomorrow.*

The list was endless. Charlotte sat on the creaky office chair and went to work.

Chapter 7

Mary rounded the corner and displayed every sign of someone becoming unhinged. Her hair had a life of its own and was in no clear decipherable style, just jutting out in corners like a starfish. Her face was distorted and sour as she trudged forward; a bull at the Spanish Bull Run comes to mind. Mary felt she was under water, couldn't breathe; sure to drown.

All week she had been subjected to coaching sessions from Sharon, the girl from the borough. She had three lesson observations this week; with very mixed reviews, and now this! Ofsted is in tomorrow.

She had had a terrible week. Sharon had dragged out the coaching sessions until five-thirty pm each afternoon, she wondered if she was being paid by the hour. She had been observed by two deputy heads and she didn't know whether she was going or coming. They kept asking her what she thought of the lesson, as if they weren't the damn observers! It infuriated her how they magnified and multiplied by ten any flaw she mentioned about the lesson and pounced like sharks that scented blood. Good God, how much could one woman take?

Everything felt like the proverbial stitch up. She was tormented, her thoughts were an army of ants which crawled under her skin and stung.

She felt an uncommon strain on her heart and wondered if a heart failure was possible at her age; the trek to the English office was monumental even though it was a journey she took daily. What lessons would she plan for year eleven tomorrow? It was hard enough getting her head round the new iGCSE exam, her class was split right down the middle; half were doing the extended paper and the others were just fit for the core-two different types of questioning. Extended and Core? What the hell happened to higher and foundation tier. Only someone sexually frustrated would name the two tiers extended and core. The wanker!

With effort and the sheer will of God, Mary made it to the office, breathless and on the brink of tears. But she was a proud woman, she was Yoruba, a chief's daughter and nobody should see her cry. She mustered the strength and braved greeting her colleagues as she makes her way to the stock cabinet at the side of the room. She needed paperclips to organise the masses of paper Sharon had given her, clearly the girl knew nothing about saving the trees. Paper clips and a few board pens in hand Mary exits the office and stands for a few seconds inhaling fresh air. She couldn't spend another minute in this hell hole, she would have to go home and prepare for the nightmare which was tomorrow.

As Mary negotiates her way through the dark alley to Upper Street on which her car is parked, she takes a tumble. She didn't see the half a brick that had lain on the dimly lit path. Her folder and the contents of her bag spill everywhere. On a vile curse, she tries to heave herself and retrieve her bits and pieces, but she is just weary - defeated. She had gathered most of her things except for a few mud-soaked scripts which were not salvageable and was ready to move on until she noticed the tub of paperclips opened with some of the contents spilt. The paperclips looked strangely beautiful and glowed even though there was hardly any light around. They had a magical quality and Mary watched fascinated, enthralled, the corners of her lips began to twitch and stretch until her teeth bared. She smiled, a smile that didn't reach her eyes as she sat down on the wet path beside the paperclips and the malodorous drain.

Slowly, almost trans-like, Mary reached for a handful of paperclips and meticulously separated them.

She dropped the first one down the drain.

She listened for the plop as it hit the bottom and when it came it was cathartic, her smile widened. She got another handful and this time dropped three paperclips down the drain, it was invigorating, and Mary felt stronger. Next, she counted ten and dropped them in, the feeling was incredible and now there was a frenzy, a mad rush as Mary threw in more and more, the smile had mutated into a chuckle and then a spine-splitting howl. Dropping the last few was practically orgasmic, and Mary stood there shaking.

Five long minutes passed before she turned to go home.

Chapter 8

THE POST OFSTED EXPERIENCE

Half the school is off sick. A quarter with diarrhoea. Management had declared this unsatisfactory and had demanded video footage. This has not however improved school attendance and I mean of the staff. The Ofsted report had arrived with inadequate stamped all over it! They were inadequate in every single area! Now everyone was up shit creek (without a paddle), one had to be double-binoculared to find any positive comments. The report was littered with comments like *"The school is **dangerous** and **unsafe**"; "The attainment in Maths and English is lagging **behind**"; The* *leadership is "**eccentric**".* In assessing teaching and learning it was noted "teachers do not routinely assess pupils' progress in lessons. They do not ask probing questions to stretch pupils' understanding or encourage engagement." As for the teaching, in general, teachers were bad surgeons who with the wrong dosage of anaesthetic had accidentally put their students into a coma. And it went on and on... No wonder bowels had been loosened.

Poor George. He had turned a nasty shade of grey, fifty shades of stress. He had been merely a mucky ghost of whom there had been infrequent citing until it was the morning to rally the troops and deliver the verdict. He didn't know where to start. Although he was, in general, a positive man, you can't pluck positivity from thin air, can you? He had cried, yes cried, something he hadn't done since the passing of his "mama". He had taken a swig of bourbon in his office, then used mouthwash to disguise any tell-tale odour. To hell with the no-alcohol rule in school, it's at times like these that it should be served in the staff canteen with lunch.

What a bloody mess.

A guru, a visit to the Spearmint Rhino couldn't even help him now. A visit to the Volupte Lounge perhaps? Nothing could stir George from the mood of absolute career ruin which lingered in the air like sour milk and rotten cabbage. The putrid smell pervaded his mind, body and threatened his soul. The noose of termination tightened around his neck, his chest had joined in the constriction. It was getting harder and harder to breathe. He wondered was it too late to find Jesus?

Little Gemma (remember her?) had tried her best to raise his mood and reassure him that she would remain loyal-under him-whatever may come. Nevertheless, he was miserable; surely he was too young to die from an aneurysm. Why did he have to choose Hades High as the starting place for his career in headship?

He looked at his staff gathered in the leaking hall and dejection, misery, cynicism and abhorrence pelted him like rocks. He couldn't stand, but he must-the troops await. The roof of his mouth is dry, and it was a struggle to engage his brain. His mouth opens though and mechanically he hears himself quoting from Churchill: "Never give in, never give in, never, never, never, never—in nothing, great or small, large or petty—never give in except to convictions of honour and good sense. Never yield to force; never yield to the apparently overwhelming might of the enemy."... His feelings checked out and his lips took control.

Charlotte sat at the back of the hall listening to George speak, or half listening rather. She was wearing all black; her body didn't need any slendering, the colour reflected her mood. She saw George's lips move but had difficulty processing anything he said. How would she respond? After a failed Ofsted people lose their jobs, get fired (no asked to leave discretely), you sometimes don't even get good references: career ruin-no holidays abroad! The mortgage! At the same minute an orange peel hits her in the neck, she has a thought.

She had to prove herself most valuable-she had to let the head know he needed her. She had worked too hard, did too much to position herself in this game of progression. She would not allow ruin to descend on her because of a grave Ofsted report. So, what did it matter if her lesson observations had been less than satisfactory on the day?

That was one of many. There had to be a way forward, had to be a way. As she roamed the corridor looking for who could be throwing orange peels at the staff, she wouldn't be surprised if it was John and Brian, they had been let back into school. She hatched a plan, and for the first time in a few days she smiled.

Chapter 9

Sean Williams is on break duty. He is in animated conversation with a cute little boy with big chestnut eyes, who speaks no English. He had lost his football or suspected one of the big year eleven boys had taken it. Quite a difficult conversation which involved a lot of pointing, gestures and hopping around. During this little transfer he thought of all his duties as a teacher:

During break he had to direct new students to their various destinations, ensure they went into the canteen in an orderly fashion, confiscate incorrect uniform, look out for all forms of bullying, spot signs of child abuse, figure out if anybody appears suicidal, identify future terrorists and those likely to run off and join IS.

After break, he would be teaching a mixed ability group of slow, average and advanced learners all preparing for the same exam, preparing lessons and photocopying worksheets-it didn't help the photocopiers were often broken –the repair technician could well do with living on campus. He would respond to all the emails from staff, students and idlers who had gotten a hold of his email address, he would fix the speakers above his whiteboard, he would find a few exemplars for the homework they had given to all students across the department-his head of department demanded it!

After school, he would call parents to report progress or problems with pupils, mark the workbooks he collected, meet with a parent who wanted to have a quick chat and spend 5 minutes with Gareth his tutee explaining why he Gareth, didn't have any friends. Then plan some more lessons and gather and make resources. And of course, pack in his man bag the work he had to take home.

On the way home, he would stop at Poundland to buy some pencils. He doubted department stock would come anytime soon.

That's a hell of a lot to do!

Which is why Sean didn't trouble himself too much, he did the little he could. As far as he was concerned the relationships he built were more important. Get on with everybody and life should be easier. Students love him, and staff will soon adore him-half the battle won really. If only he could get some people to look past the fact that he was a mixed-race man with an English mother and a Jamaican father.

He was never going to let all this tension about the disastrous Ofsted report bother his sweet cheeks. The overarching sense of panic, doom and gloom hanging in the air had to be repelled. There were people to meet, conversations to be had, he had no time for drama.

Chapter 10

Ninety-five percent of the teaching staff is working like slaves. When have they never? But in the wake of the nastiest Ofsted report known to man, their efforts have been doubled. A few more are off (with diarrhoea) but the majority of staff is now practically living in school. There were many changes afoot and the rumours had begun.

George has been given a mentor, the head teacher of a neighbouring school. Despite the bruise to his ego, he embraced it. If Bingham held the key to turning this sinking ship around, not only would he be his saviour but his friend for life. He was no fool. George knew he was in dire straits, a catch 22, in a vicious cycle and grasping at straws-the idioms could continue. However, he must plod on, if he was allowed to. There were already rumours of a possible termination: of course; he wouldn't give credence to that.

He would learn, he would become better, he would improve but the crux of the matter (idiom overload) was he was faced with incompetence at all angles. At least, he had expected the teachers he had observed and given his seal of approval prior to Ofsted to have good lesson observations, or at least members of the senior staff, i.e., his assistant and deputy heads. But like a bolt from the blue, they were shit! The credibility gap. Who would believe his judgements now? Where do you go when your deputy head, in charge of staff training fails? Not one, but two Ofsted lesson observations over the two and a half days those bloodsucking ghouls, masquerading as assessors were in school.

OK, the thought occurred to him to keep this all silent, but how could he, when the said deputy head in charge of staff training was observed by all who happened to pass at the moment of feedback, crying and wailing on the floor, balls outstretched, for all and sundry to crunch.

Areas in the school which he had deemed to have improved weren't even acknowledged in the report. The long and short of it, there were catastrophic failings. He had trusted the wrong people on reflection. He remembered all the flashy promises; the high percentage passes departments were expecting, the useful links people had with other institutions both local and abroad which would be beneficial to the school. Everything looked bleak now he was royally rogered. He knew the school needed change but who could he trust to help him with the turnaround?

He thought of his wife and their life. She hadn't thought it was a good idea to take up this post, perhaps she had been on to something. When he had thought about moving on to a new challenge this wasn't what he had in mind. Of course, he would see the kids less, and of course he would be home later not always making dinner, and of course he had to be prepared to be criticised more by colleagues and staff, but he hadn't anticipated this. The sacrifice he had initially thought was worth it. After all the family would have more money, longer and better holidays, more respect in their little village, he would be in the news occasionally and the children could be privately educated. Plus, the power. The power. Being a headteacher was a powerful position you just needed to stop yourself short of being too "trumpesque". So, he had taken her on a short holiday to Spain-not the budget side where people who found deals on the internet stayed, but a charming little villa by the sea, not too near, or too far from where they planned to film the reality TV spin-off, Ibiza Shore.

After the weekend she had been in full agreement with him taking up the post and promised to support him in any way she could, but he hadn't anticipated this. To be fraught with making plans and changes, to have council officials breathing down your neck, to have parents shouting "you're rubbish" down the phone, to have colleagues from his previous schools ring to express their sympathy at recent events in the most unsympathetic tone; but the absolute worst, was the cold clawing fingers of self-doubt whose caress intensified with each passing hour.

He had never doubted himself till now.

Hard decisions will have to be made, he had to save the school and he had to save himself –who employed a failed head? Oh, to get rid of the scorpions in his mind. His body trembled, and he knew what he needed, he needed Gemma, her enthusiasm and wealth of ideas were what he needed now. Her fervour was enough to improve his mood and strip him naked of his fears.

He had no doubt he would be roused after their quick meeting. He would ask his PA to send for her immediately, even if she was teaching; he would provide cover. He looked forward to a revival and the energy to fight another day.

Chapter 11

It's Monday morning and rain clouds have gathered over the school. This is a real worry because many sections of the building are leaking. There is a hole at the back of the main office just below the broken gutter and water and anything else lurking in the gutters run right into the office when it rains, and trickles down the steps into the main classrooms and under the carpets. The stench is unbearable, and the cleaners discover the real meaning of hell. Imagine soaked carpets, unwashed PE kits in lockers and half-eaten cheese and tuna sandwiches stuffed into corners, all in one room.

Lightning has struck the school too and asses have been singed. Well not literally, but to say it simply, people are feeling the heat. The tension in the corridors is a physical force and is now as real as bricks and mortar. People speak in whispers and all conversations are now confidential.

People have sharpened up their dress; Howard had taken to wearing a dark suit. He wasn't very pleased on Friday when Christopher asked him who had died and if the funeral was right after school. People were in school at the crowing of the cock. In fact, you often wondered if some people had actually gone home the previous night. A new and unexpected phenomenon had also broken out in the school, something many staff hadn't encountered since their teenage years.

Acne.

Oily and acneic skin triggered by hormones was now a common citing. Apparently, acne can occur at any stage in our lives, the primary aggravating factor leading to adult acne though is chronic stress. We all know that acute stress can cause a breakout from time to time, as chronic, continual stress increases hormone levels, which can lead to an increase in oil production.

Oil is pouring.

So, it doesn't help that the staff is now greasy, fatigued and prone to diarrhoea.

The borough has offered psychiatric help, and all teaching staff have been given little cards the size of a credit card with a number they could call discretely if for any reason they felt they were overwhelmed or even slightly suicidal. Many a staff had looked at the wording at the top **"Need somebody to talk to?"** and after longing stares had stuffed it back into their purses and wallets. It probably wasn't wise to call.

Weight gain.

Fat was stalking the teaching staff and was attaching itself to the most unlikely of places and the most unlikely people. The new healthy eating menu now being served to everyone in the school canteen wasn't looking effective. The staff wanted, needed, sugar and fried food to get them through the days.

Brenda, woman of the people, had been to the Bonmarché sales twice and had invested in many a striped top, two sizes up. There was one embarrassing trouser tearing episode in MFL (Modern Foreign Language) where fat had wrestled itself free through the seams of one trouser leg and the teacher wasn't quick enough to shield it from thirty pairs of scandalous eyes and quick cameras. It was all over Facebook and Instagram.

George hadn't been in school for a week. He was off on training somewhere abroad.

Chapter 12

Mary turns the key in her north London flat. She is immediately enfolded in gospel music and a strong smell. She sniffs the air and eventually recognises the odour, it is 62.8% white overproof rum. By the window half wrapped in her Ikea curtains is Adebola, her husband. He hears her hesitant footsteps and turns slowly. His initial expression of euphoria and bewilderment morphs into a slow lazy smile. He takes a step towards her and releases the curtain in which he was draped, he sways a little to the right but stands facing his wife in his Matalan Y-front briefs.

Mary resigns herself to another episode.

'Hi', she manages.

'Hello, my sweet wife' he counters in a half slur. He seems to find his feet, and juts towards her and grabs her in a bear hug, his skin sticking to her like a bad adhesive.

Initially she doesn't respond but then gathers her strength and places her arms around him. He notes the tension in her body and stuffs her into his chest and puts his head on her shoulders.

They stand together for a few minutes... and then another few, it is then she notes that Adebola is getting heavier. She begins to feel a warm trickle down her back soaking into her orange polyester top and jerks Adebola from his little inertia. He battles to open his eyes and wins; he steps back from her embrace and smiles.

Mary turns her back and walks away, a shield against her emotions, and tries to establish some sense of normalcy through conversation.

'There is talk of termination at school, more specifically, my termination.

Adebola's eyes widen dramatically and his lips move swiftly.

'Matthew 24 verse 6, and ye shall hear of wars and rumours of wars: see that ye be not troubled: for all these things must come to pass, but the end is not yet.'

She ignores his response and carries on.

'Apparently my practice is veering on "inadequate performance."

'And who determines this? The battle is the Lords!'

'Apparently there are five grounds related to job performance concerns for which you can be dismissed: inadequate performance, neglect of duty, failure to fulfil the statutory duties of a teacher, insubordination and failure to comply with the reasonable requirements of the board. Apparently, I fall into one of them.' It's all laid out in Grounds for Dismissal under the Teacher Tenure Act.

Despite the strange fuzziness in his head Adebola forced himself to listen as Mary spoke, he let her pour her heart out and offload the burdens she felt and faced, occasionally the anguish behind her words connected with him; but didn't linger.

'Do you think the awful Ofsted report is the cause of all this?'

Finally! Mary felt a tinge of happiness at the question; she was desperate for his true engagement.

'Well that certainly played a factor.'

Mary recalled the events of her lesson observation by the Ofsted inspector and marvelled at how unlucky she was. She had been under such scrutiny and pressure internally that she really didn't fancy a visit from the all-powerful top dogs. It was the last timetabled session before the inspection was meant to conclude and everyone could just about hold in the tension, one more session and many would burst into deflation like a balloon at the end of a birthday party. But there was only one period to go and soon they would be in the clear. Her lesson has started, and she had managed to get all the children into the room without much incident, it was now ten minutes into the lesson and they were mostly subdued, she had just about managed to give out her first worksheet when there was an ominous creak of the door, and a man walked in.

He wore a silver suit and was quite tall. A white shirt complemented the suit with a bright silky looking red tie with very subtle dots. His face was fairly thin and so were his lips the periphery of which were etched thin lines. He had the clearest glasses she had ever seen, in fact if it wasn't for the necessary frame, from a little distance you would miss that he was wearing glasses altogether. He slithered in with little eye contact and stalked to the nearest empty chair, sat down beside Brian and she knew she was doomed. It also didn't help that Claire, a feisty little firecracker whom she had given a detention the previous week immediately put up her hand. Mary knew she was up to no good, but Claire couldn't be ignored, Mary could feel the eyes of the inspector piercing her and willing her to respond. With a great feeling of doom and in her best voice Mary had said

'Yes Claire?'

And Claire with the face of an angel and a voice to match smiled and said,

'I'm surprised we have a worksheet today miss and a coloured one at that, we never have anything prepared. Pink is my favourite colour. Well done.'

Things only went downhill from then.

Adebola listened to his wife as best as he could and walked to her turned back and slumped shoulders, he embraced her from behind and let his hold linger. He held her gently for a few moments and let her feel the weight of his sympathy, and then he whispered ever so serenely,

'I know what you need. I can help. Let's have a baby.' Mary's next thought was one of murder.

Chapter 13

Charlotte is wearing sky blue. Her blouse has theatrical ruffles to the front with long sheer sleeves. The pencil skirt makes her seem thinner than she actually is although her pockets stick out giving the impression of slight curves. This little ensemble is complemented with tan court shoes. She is wearing unusual amounts of makeup and quite frankly she whiffs a bit, or could it be the toilets? After all she is standing in the corridors just by the male lavatory. She is on break duty and is standing just below a poorly drawn penis, the work of some clever student.

Charlotte isn't on the official list for duty on a Tuesday but thought it would be a good idea to be visible, to help out, to prove just a little bit harder just how much she was worth. She was determined to emerge victorious through troubled times. The troubles that's what she would call it, just like what her gran spoke about in Northern Ireland; the troubles, because in truth the school had turned into a war zone. Ill-will was now commonplace; people had formed dodgy alliances-staff who hadn't spoken regularly or even in years were now best of friends; allies during the troubles. Enemies now bonded over a fag and lunch breaks. In certain respects, Charlotte had observed what could only be described as the gathering of the clans. Clans of all creeds and colours and motives. There was without doubt territorial conflict.

But Charlotte was a fighter, a real warrior and would not be daunted, despite the odds. It is why she was positioned where she was, it's why her pockets were bulkier today, and it's why she was on duty. If you can't beat them, join them, for your own benefit of course. She wondered how many casualties there would be in this round of conflict.

Charlotte was jolted from her thoughts when George emerged, right on her hopeful schedule, from the toilet.

Let the games begin.

Her lips spread wide and teeth bared in what should be a smile.

'Hello George' she chirped.

He seemed to notice her for the first time and turned with a weird expression on his face she couldn't read. He seemed bewildered or irritated, perhaps discombobulated. It was hard to tell.

'Hi Charlotte' he responded. She hoped it wasn't a tone of boredom she detected.

'It's fortunate meeting you here, although you must be in a rush but...'

'Yes, I've got a meeting.'

'Oh, I won't take much of your time. I'm not insensitive I know there must be so much you have to do, but something you said in our last meeting resonated with me, and I realised how I could help.'

'What were you thinking Charlotte?'

'I can see the mood of the staff, and I hear things, and people aren't always supportive. Some people have clearly given up, but I think there is a fight to be fought and we can bounce back to former glory.'

George restrained himself from a sardonic" What former glory?" response and arched an eyebrow.

Charlotte detected some interest and pursued what little of it she could grab.

'We have had such negative talk in the local community, and even nationally, we've got to counteract this. What we need is positive publicity to improve our image, raise the profile of the school and become credible in the community again.'

'I suppose that goes without saying.'

'Well I can help; I've got good contacts with the press, particularly the local newspaper.'

The words were rushing from her mouth now and her brain was ticking over fast-she felt uncommon adrenaline and a feeling of anticipation was rising threatening to consume her whole body.

'I'm sure I can come up with positive things they can say about the school. Let me bounce some ideas around and tell you what I come up with.'

'Yes Charlotte, you are thinking in the right direction. Create a plan and a get back to me, but I really must dash now. Email me if you must.'

'Okay George I won't delay and will inform you soon.', she said as sultrily as she could, complemented with a wink. By this time, she was talking to his back as he'd lengthened his strides, eager to get away.

As if on cue the break bell rang, but Charlotte stood there for a little while longer. She suddenly felt...odd. She couldn't quite tell whether she'd scored a victory or not. He seemed mildly interested but strangely distant.

Charlotte shook it off. She would call Grant her old friend. Surely, he hadn't forgotten that one night in Dubai; he was editor-in-. chief now and of course he owed her a favour.

Chapter 14

George entered his office and slammed the door shut. He leaned on the back of it and allowed his shoulders to slump, his head to fall and just to be loose-limbed for a minute. It was a temporary way to relieve stress. Seeking relief from stress was now a pastime for him. It seemed he couldn't leave his office without being attacked one way or another. Everybody wanted to speak to him, everybody had a great idea or wanted to help, now Charlotte, but sadly they just seemed to add salt to the wound.

Brenda thought it necessary to represent the feelings of the staff and kept sending him emails with the most inappropriate smileys. The HOYS were upset because he demanded closer monitoring and accountability for each year group and that they stayed on the premises till 5 in the evenings. The HODS were upset because he wanted weekly monitoring and reports of the progress of the exam groups; The PE faculty was annoyed because he had pulled funding for some of the extracurricular activities as there was a hole in the budget. The cleaners thought it was unreasonable that he asked for tables and chairs to be wiped each day with a home-made mixture, part water, part vinegar and part lemon juice. He had arranged new in-house training opportunities for the teaching staff. He expected everyone to attend at least one training session each week. The unions had a problem with that; but so what? If their members hadn't been so ineffective to start with the school wouldn't be in its current dilemma!

The borough was not happy with his action plan. He had spent many late afternoons, and nights, formulating an action plan, consulting others, yet they were not satisfied. It's not that they had an issue with some of his ideas; he expected that, he accepted he wasn't perfect, but by God, they had a problem with every bullet point. In his estimation the nit-picking was unnecessary. This fussy pedantic fault-finding was just bullshit.

He had missed his son's recital. After a few years of insisting he did piano lessons and grounding him the times he had absconded, his son had finally got to a place where he could play publicly. His son had played at their school assembly to which parents were invited and he had not been able to attend. His son hadn't quite forgiven him yet. His wife who was always a picture of support had gone frosty; he couldn't tell exactly why!

He had never had so many complaints from parents in his whole life. Parents who had been indifferent to their children's performance for years were now unhappy with the quality and quantity of their children's homework; he was being asked about children's safety and about the locking of the school gates. One parent after screaming at him a load of expletives, told him to go back to where he came from how he had ruined the school and that a woman should be the head teacher because men were all "shit."

It was needless to say George could do well with some quick improvements in his life, being a cashier at Lidl was appearing far more attractive than being a head teacher.

Life had to get better.

Chapter 15

The crack in the wall near the science block is bigger, a few more bricks had fallen out this week and it appears more like a gaping hole now rather than a crevice. The children were stuffing all sorts of goods through there from friends outside. The school is littered with chicken and chips boxes and sweet wrappers of all types were a common feature of the décor. It wasn't unusual to come upon one or two empty beer cans and a half-smoked spliff. For those who loved rats, this was the place to be. They ran freely about in broad daylight. The cleaners had a hell of a job.

But there were reasons to smile this week. A ray of hope. The usual hush was in the staff room when Brenda burst in smiling from ear to ear. The school had been in the local and national papers again this week, but for a good reason; she had copies of both publications.

'Has anybody seen this?' she asked, loud enough to engage anyone who would care to respond.

'Seen what?' Howard who was sitting at the back near the old photocopier queried.

'The articles' Brenda bellowed. She was met with a few grunts and one nod.

'Isn't this great?' 'We've been having such a hard time, so much has been said about us as a school, that it has been discouraging and depressing. But this is great, this is wonderful, certainly it marks a turning point of how the public sees us and acknowledges the hard work we have put into these kids over the years. I mean things might not be at their best now, but we have had many successes, many noteworthy accomplishments over the years. It is those years of success that we mustn't forget, we can be good again, and we can be great again. Look at the former glory!'

Brenda's voice had risen to a shriek with its depth of emotion. She paused to catch her breath and waited for her colleagues to respond. One person started a slow steady clap; another visibly raised an eyebrow, the other three returned to their bowl- soup of the day –with crusty bread-served in the canteen.

Brenda began to process things in slow motion; she saw the turned backs, the sarcasm, the indifference, and truly knew for the first time in her life what it meant to be crestfallen. Tears pooled in her eyes, she allowed her body to act until her mind and spirit could catch up. One shaking hand gripped the two news articles, the other wiped a tear trying to save her dignity. Luckily her feet co-operated to put one in front of the other and turned towards the door.

As Brenda exits her fingers clutch the articles then crunches them into a ball. The one that was a frontpage splash was written by a Grant Penn who in his article spoke about the success of the school's debating team in the most embellished, exaggerated vocabulary possible, and also their penfriend programme. The article hailed the vision and foresight of the school who in their bid to provide a sense of stability and wholeness had started the pen pal initiative to reassure and comfort their huge population of migrant children. This programme was deeply academically rooted. Apparently, it was inspired by a story on the AQA English Literature syllabus whereby a Polish school cleaner found her roots and regained her self-esteem by having been a pen friend to the new head teacher or something of the sort.

These children were encouraged and given the opportunity to write to students in other countries and their own homeland to bond and share experiences through which they could become one, leading to more emotionally stable and well-adjusted children. One lucky pupil would be allowed to travel to meet the penfriend with their family, if it was a safe destination and could be arranged by the adults, with some expenses paid for by the school. The article didn't mention that so far no one had ever gone to meet their pen pal.

Chapter 16

A bird is perched in the year nine office, its shifty blue eyes are glazed and sparkling, and it is gently swaying as if being blown by a mellow Caribbean breeze. Every now and then it prunes its feathers and stretches its wings wide, then refolds them tight around her belly. Its upper and lower mandible are spread to reveal slightly yellow, faintly discoloured teeth. Her smile is wide even her third molar can be seen. Charlotte is ecstatic; she is feeling immeasurable pleasure, a cathartic effect from the news she has received. Everything was going to plan.

Grant had kept to his word and given her the front-page splash. Her work with the debating team and her penfriend programme was all over the front page of the local newspaper; it was the much-needed positive publicity that the school desired; from all accounts the head teacher was very impressed! He had been modest in his response to her accomplishment, but those close to him knew he was delighted by what she had done. She knew that as the head he couldn't show too much emotion, it was a feature of the job that he be stoic. In fact, she contemplated that he was probably desperate to hug her but couldn't. he had to consider the implications for other staff and guard against jealousy. Surely now everyone must be covetous of how he would view her. He would have to be retarded not to recognise how beneficial she was and could be to the school. Surely, he could see her loyalty to him and the institution, how impassioned she was about the school making a turnaround, she could see another headline in her future something along the lines of how she spearheaded the triumph against adversity, to help to lead her school to success, to be the envy of all the other schools in the borough.

Charlotte allowed another wave of bliss to wash over her, she leaned back, closed her eyes again and let the jubilation stroke her body to a pinnacle from which she didn't want to descend. These were the moments one lived for, the glimpse of greatness on the horizon, the hints of a successful career, and she took a moment to reflect.

Her plans might have been calculated but this was the way forward, these were modern times and you couldn't just wait around to fall into a career or allow things to happen to you, that was old thinking! To progress in your career you need favour, you have to impress the right people and be connected to those who have some clout. You need to reassure those who have huge responsibilities and projects, that you could be their Benjamin, their right-hand child. She often complimented senior staff on what they wore.

Charlotte chuckled to herself, she had been a bit naughty recently and had invested in a Sony ICD-PX333 handheld voice recorder, and it was often in her pocket. She smirked at her deception and had to marvel at how she came up with these ingenious ideas. You would be surprised how many people she had recorded, how many conversations she had on her little device.

People had spilt their guts to her about their frustrations about how things were in the school, how they felt about George and what they blamed him for, others had cunning plans about how they would leave and seek employment elsewhere. One person confessed how her personal doctor was also a good friend and he would soon diagnose her with something big, really big, rendering her unfit for work for quite a long time, anything she needed to get away from this mess. She had many a priceless recording, but she wasn't nasty-she had only ever used one. Yes, one teacher from the PE department that she hadn't particularly liked had disappeared under hushed circumstances; apparently a little someone was able to secure a little recording of her haranguing poor George. She had vented with fulminating rancour how she felt about George cutting the department budget, and the demands he had made on the teaching staff, she had outlined her plans for covert insubordination, she had eventually ended her little tirade by calling him "a floating turd".

Charlotte couldn't suppress a chuckle; actually, she allowed it to intensify into full-blown laughter, echoing in the office coming back to her like a supportive friend.

Chapter 17

The corridor is noisier than usual, mostly because music is blasting from one of the classrooms on the right. Clean Bandit and Jess Glynne's *"Rather Be"* could be heard all around, it seemed to be stuck on the chorus" no nuh no no, no place I'd rather be".

The irony.

It was too loud to ignore so George on his patrol had stuck his head in to see what on earth was going on. He was met with a scene that he wasn't sure he could describe.

At the door he was greeted by torn wall displays tossed on the ground and a smashed globe. Some lights were on, but the room was dark enough for visibility to be impaired. A bale of lined paper was used to carpet a section of the floor and tables and chairs had been pushed back against the walls. The whiteboard was clean except for a few badly drawn balloons and a machine gun in the middle. Scribbled at the side was a tag followed by faint scribblings "was ere".

Two girls were standing on the paper-lined section of the floor which George now recognised as a dancefloor. They were not wearing school uniform or perhaps their own versions of it. The school shirts were not tucked into their skirts as they should be; but were tied in bows just under their breasts, they wore skimpy pleated skirts which were miles shorter than the uniform rules allowed, each wore knee-high striped socks. If he hadn't known better he would have thought they were epileptic, they shook and jutted themselves at odd angles.

There were about 15 other students in the room, drinking and eating sweets, there was a smell of burgers. Burgers! Where would children find burgers at 11 o clock in the morning? He let rip an authoritative shout, to no avail. He looked again at the label on the door to ensure he made a note of the room. He would check the timetable to see which teacher should be there at this time. Someone would have to explain why this class was left unmanned, somebody or several somebodies heads would roll! It clearly states in the teachers' duty of the care that a credentialed teacher must be in the classroom with students at all times. Somehow George knew by the end of the week he would be at least one teaching staff less.

He turned to leave when a shuffling at the back caught his eye. Out of the darkness from the rear of the classroom stripes bubbled forward and Brenda slowly emerged. George was shocked, too shocked to utter a word. He and Brenda made eye contact and he saw her, truly saw her like he hadn't seen her before. He whispered as softly as possible, 'I'll see you later' and turned to exit.

Chapter 18

Sean Williams is depressed and insecure. He wasn't quite sure why. He knew he was sad because his good friend had died in the recent mass shooting and bomb attack in Paris. He couldn't get the atrocity out of his mind. Who does that sort of a thing? What depraved, immoral human being could see innocent life and just snatch it. The only crime his friend had committed was to attend a concert.

Sean was sad.

He didn't feel any joy in going to work either. Each day he entered a place which appeared like death had warmed over, people didn't smile in the corridor anymore, his casual conversations were being rebuffed, and the staff room was like a ghost town, there was hardly anybody there. Nearly everybody is fat! He'd always kept himself trim and found it difficult to tolerate obesity. Gone were the lively chats about football matches, the news headlines, the ineffectiveness of government policies, who was building an extension, the last concert somebody attended, the holiday someone had taken that they were desperate for the whole staff to know about. Gone were the chats about students and their parents, the odd nutter here and there. Gone was the idle critique of colleagues' competence behind their backs. It was all gone. What had stolen the soul of the school? It was almost as if people were afraid to talk, to open their mouths and speak; but actually, they weren't, because replacing these lively perhaps meaningless chats were rumours. Yes, rumours.

Did you hear that Brenda was off getting psychiatric help? Did you know that Mary was going to be sacked for incompetence? Have you heard they were looking to cut teaching staff and a coven was formed which gathered at night looking for loopholes in employment contracts as grounds for dismissal? Did you hear that one teacher who was supposed to be off sick with a severe episode of diarrhoea had actually returned to school too tanned and too relaxed? Did you hear that TLR (Teaching and Learning Responsibility) points were being seized and redistributed among a certain clique? Did you know that George was sleeping with... the rumours were endless.

All the cleaners were whispering again. It was just too unbelievable. They had witnessed George Nobbs and Sean exchanging strong words with matching facial expressions. Apparently, a parent had called to complain that he was not marking books. Claire's mother had called first then wrote an email to the headteacher and the governors, then soon after that a barrage of parents followed suit.

Apparently, the conversation went something like this.

'This cannot continue!' George was said to have shouted.

'The school has enough problems to deal with without adding this basic level of incompetence to it all.'

'I am hurt that this is how things have been interpreted.' Sean had responded.

'What do you mean by that!' George had ripped back. 'Well I think of myself as a teacher who gives the children just what they need and that is what I thought I was doing.'

'I don't follow you.'

'Well look at the atmosphere. Look at how tense and uncertain things have been in our school. We constantly expect disaster and people have been physically ill because of it, I don't want this to happen to my students.'

The headteacher had apparently just grunted and not responded. Sean had continued.

'I have relaxed things for my students, I don't demand as much as I used to, I'm sure research would agree that keeping them under this constant tension, driving them to work continuously like slaves and extending that into homework would be to the detriment of pupils, not to mention me marking books and assessing them, applying pressure is not how we should operate.'

Apparently the headteacher was mute. Sean continued.

'The key is getting parents to understand this and appreciate this new strategy. It's like having an army on high-alert, always expecting danger, tense and wary. After a few months they would be completely exhausted and disillusioned and then no good to anyone ever again, can't you see? Stringent marking and monitoring are a danger to their mental health.'

Apparently the headteacher had walked off.

But that was not the only thing the cleaners were whispering about.

Apparently, there was a strange smell coming from the headteachers' office in the afternoon. The cleaners had been trying to decipher the source. It smelt like a combination of many things but a bit hard to determine. It was like a strange perfume but with a kind of smoky consistency. The air freshener they used could not completely mask the smell and it often lingered after they had finished cleaning. It was the strangest thing. It was not only until one Thursday afternoon that the mystery was solved. George Nobbs was leaving early, both he and little Gemma had hurriedly left the office. The cleaners arrived shortly after to the smell and a small tray with perfume, incense and an incomplete spliff. Apparently the headteacher was on the weed. Apparently.

The whispers continued

The school had entered children in the National Variety Competition which meant they had to journey to Wales and stay overnight. Apparently, it was only after returning that they realised they had left one student behind. They were trying desperately to keep this information out of the local news. Apparently.

There was even a rumour about him, his perceptible lack of commitment to the job. Now that was laughable! Who was more suitable for this job than he? He was in school every day, he was friendly. He had broken up fights because the children listened to him. He was sure if they did a survey of who had the most conversations with students and staff of all departments it would be him. He had organised a few pub crawls for staff. So, what if his lesson during the Ofsted inspection hadn't gone to plan? Or that he had missed the odd deadline every now and then. So what if he didn't always set homework or stick to the department marking policy? So what if his exam results weren't as good as they could be for the past two years? So what? He was the life of the school, no one could deny his presence and what he brought, he was fun to talk to and helped people to relax-these were all essentials. Do people really understand how difficult the life of a teacher really is? Don't they understand that to be a teacher is to be a: counsellor, paramedic, parent, security guard, forensic detective, editor, inventor, communicator, toiletries provider and a fashion victim?

But he was sad.

Perhaps now was a good time to settle down and get married, he knew he wanted children of his own. He had battled hard to get from under the shadow of being a product of a black father and a white mother and he had done well despite the exclusions. Yes, now was the time to start creating his own family, being at home would be a better atmosphere than being at school, he would have something to look forward to each day. It was time to find a wife; there were other things of importance in this life than a good career. It was time to find a wife. He wanted a white one of course. It was time to rewrite the wrongs.

Chapter 19

The staff is burdened beyond measure, to bear the constant pressure to perform to improve and not to have it recognised was humanly impossible to maintain. It didn't help that they were sheep without a shepherd, as George had not been in school for over a week again. He had had a mild heart attack.

George's little ticker nearly clogged out, but he was still alive. The previous week there was an early morning call from his wife to say he had been hospitalised and she couldn't predict at this point how long he would be out of school. She suspected recent events had been too much for him and had placed an unnecessary strain on his heart.

The truth is, George had received some terrible news. The governors had spoken, and they wanted him gone. They had shamed his action plan as short-sighted and generally suggested he had no vision. It was a wound from which George doubted he could recover. He had seen the looks of doubt and distrust in the eyes of his own staff. He had suffered abuse from parents when he stood outside in the mornings as they dropped off their children, he had colleagues from his former school phoning to express sympathy, in the most ingenuine tones.

How could he recover from this? What reputation would he have going forward? Who would employ him? Where was his credibility? He envisioned career ruin. To have worked so hard in a profession for years and end up on the scrap heap, he couldn't take it.

When he had gotten the phone call from the governors his first response was one of shock, then a feeling of total desolation encapsulated him until his skin began to burn. His mind was a landmine and he feared the next thought would make him explode. His body shivered. Once the cloud had faded a little, he had called his wife and given her the news, he then composed an email, and then he had sent for Gemma, he needed help. He needed a release.

She had come with her usual freshness, her usual sweetness and devotion and he allowed himself to drown in her for a while. She whispered in his ear all the reassurance that he needed, even if he didn't believe it; it was good for him, for now. He just relaxed and let it be.

She was willing and receptive to his every command; she demonstrated an obedience he wished all his staff would and George slowly began to unwind. Each button that was undone drove him further to comfort and release, he was enchanted.

But not too enchanted to hear his office door creak, to turn in time to see the cleaner with his mop and bucket in hand and a grin. Standing behind him his dejected wife. She had stopped all she had planned for the day, and had come to support him, as she had always done.

Chapter 20

The streets are dark and autumn leaves are scattered everywhere. It's only 6 o'clock but it's pitch black. It's quiet except for the police siren wailing in the distance. The occasional shape of someone wearing a hoodie lurched in a corner, or the curls of smoke from a shadowed body are all features of Mary's walk as she heads home. The walk is as usual, uneventful, till Mary notices movement on the pavement; closer inspection shows it's a crab. Instinctively she thought a crab was most unexpected in that area at that time of night, but she notices how it scuttles along the sidewalk, sideways, or perhaps diagonally would be more apt to describe it. Mary was in no hurry to get home so didn't think it idle to stop and watch it for a bit, with its short abrupt burst of speed; quick anxious steps. She wondered how it came to be out there, alone.

Thoughts of crabs together crossed her mind. Ever noticed crabs in a barrel or bucket? Ever noticed the painstaking crawl they try to make to the top against the slippery surface of the container, freedom just in sight? Ever noticed how as they struggle closer to the top, to escape, their journey is always cut short as they are clutched by another crab dragging them back down to the point where they started, at the bottom of the bucket. Nothing is accomplished, nothing is achieved, and somebody gets hurt.

Mary thought about her school and made the analogy, at least that's how she saw it. There was no togetherness, she didn't see people there, more like bloodsucking muckrakers, backstabbers, self-promoters petrified by a terrible Ofsted report, people who feared the deterioration of their lifestyles so grew fangs and made a pastime of using them, soldiers in a doleful army starring in their own versions of "Kill or be killed." For Mary it seemed time to move on, to try another profession perhaps, for she was surely losing her soul.

Mary walked on feeling tired as she approached the adjacent street on which she lived. She could see her door from where she was and slowed as she approached, her feet developed their own hesitance, unsure of what each step forward would bring them to when she eventually opened her door. It was a hard life being poked from all sides; not wanting to go to work; the hostility and feelings of fear were too strong, not wanting to come home to engulfing disappointment and neglect.

As Mary entered her home she braced herself and prepared to put on the usual bravado and fake cheerfulness necessary for her to survive. She wondered what Adebola was up to this time. She puts away her keys and sniffs the air to see what type of alcohol she could detect.

Nothing.

She listened for music, his movement, or greeting as he acknowledged her arrival.

Nothing.

She glanced in the kitchen and it was immaculate, no dishes had been used and left strewn across the counter and in the sink. No alcohol was spilt on the floor.

The bin was empty and freshly scrubbed.

It was then that Mary began to panic and ran to the bedroom fearing the worst, tears had already started to form in her eyes and a dull ache commenced in her chest, she dreaded the findings that the bedroom must produce, and her heart stopped when she saw the lump in the duvet.

She lurched towards the body praying to God he was still alive, and stopped abruptly; he wasn't there, the duvet was just lying in lumps. She peered over the other side of the bed to see if he had fallen out and was in a coma on the floor, the floor was vacant. Mary stopped in mid grief. Where was Adebola? He rarely went out.

Mary retraced her steps with a final thought to check the bathroom; it was then that she noticed the note left for her on the dining table. It read:

My darling wife Mary,

I know you have been having a tough time lately and my heart grieves for you, but don't forget as the Scriptures says"
Weeping may endure for a night but

joy cometh in the morning. I see your heartache and I question whether I have been the best husband I could be, but I love you and I know you love me too. So I vow to change my ways and today is a new beginning, a fresh start. Notice how clean the flat is? I bet that put a smile on your face. I'm MIA because I want to be the best I can be for you starting with employment. So, I am out with a friend discussing the best way forward for auditioning for Britain's Got Talent next year. Greatness is on the horizon my darling.

Your one true love,
Adebola.

Mary sat with the note in her hand not sure whether to laugh or cry. One reaction won over the other though, and tears trickled slowly down her face.

Chapter 21

SOMETHING THAT HAPPENED

The assistant head is flushed and in agony, there is a crisis. Almost as disastrous as the bad Ofsted. The black woman had won the staff sweepstake. Christ Jesus! How could this be? This had danger written all over it, the end of an era, the destruction of a deep-rooted staff tradition. This one happening could single-handedly devastate an already fractured staff.

It was the tradition at Hades High to have a staff sweepstake for major international and European competitions, be it, Five Nations Rugby, The World Cup,

The European Cup, and staff could place their bets for only one pound. At the end of the competition the winner would be announced in dramatic fashion in a staff meeting, which would be met with whoops and cheers and plans to meet up at the pub. Now the black woman had won.

It couldn't be allowed to happen. She was so unfriendly, never smiling, frank speaking and didn't understand the rules about courting the power. There is no way she could take home the staff's hard-earned money with that ass. The woman didn't even drink for goodness sake. Which teacher didn't like getting pissed on the weekends in order to face the coming week? Plus, she was ever so bloody critical of everything and everyone. Not many people had personally heard her, but Charlotte had already told them all that they needed to know.

Imagine implying that the headteacher had given a dickmotion to the skinny little girl who was now Head of Department. Imagine insisting that children should actually be made accountable for their own work or lack thereof, and not staff. Imagine telling staff that their policies and ideas were a pain in her ass, yes that ass. Imagine befriending the cleaners and the people who didn't matter. Imagine turning up in a suit and she was not even a manager or in charge of anything. Imagine working part-time, turning up three days a week and then having that super long weekend. Didn't she understand that it didn't matter if she had worked many years as a slave, a part-time teaching post was reserved for the privileged? Rumour had it that she was taunting staff with pictures on social media. She had a selfie, with her children, in the park at 5:04 pm last Tuesday when everybody else was still at work! The black woman was just too much. She even wore designer perfume mid-week!

It puzzled staff how the children liked her; there was nothing even remotely likeable about her, at least not anything that anyone with good breeding could appreciate. This winning was highly improper and needed damage control.

For a minute he panicked, then a calm came over him like being overshadowed by the Holy Ghost. He was the assistant head after all. He had been on many management courses including "The Art of Managerial Lying and Deception". He would just get someone else to assume the position of the sweepstake winner, that wouldn't be too hard. There were many people who would do as he said.

Crisis averted.

Why had he even panicked in the first place? What had made him so uncomfortable? What had pricked at his conscience? All questions he couldn't answer. It never occurred to him that the black woman understood political decisions. It never occurred to him she didn't like smiling because she hated all things fake, and her smile was slow, sincere and seductive, inappropriate for school.

He went to see his colleague typing away at the front desk.

Chapter 22

The last thing Charlotte expected when she got out of bed this morning at 5:45 am was that it would be one of the worst days of her life. Things had been going so well. Despite the clear despondency her colleagues wore so well, she had been quite buoyant in spirits. Her star could not be shining brighter since the newspaper article which was widely discussed across all realms of the school. She had been ear-marked as a game changer, the woman to help with the much-needed turnaround, the one to help build bridges in the community and wipe the events of the bad past away from their memory. She knew, although he hid it well, George was pleased with her in so many ways. She blushed every time she thought of it. Now he would be in clear support of her progress, she was glad she had found favour in his eyes and at least in the reshuffling he would see that she would make a good, dependable assistant headteacher. Charlotte quivered at the thought of the promotion. She would be half-way to her dream; to the average man, at the moment, it would seem like a huge jump from being deputy head of year to be an assistant headteacher, but surely Kim would soon be gone. In the interim period she would be head of year until she naturally progressed to an assistant head. Charlotte had dreamt about it so many times, even last night.

On her first morning after promotion she would wear red. Yes red! Red suggested passion and that she was ready to take charge. It also implied danger for those who might secretly think they wouldn't support her. She would wear higher heels that day, that would take her to about 6feet, seeing she was already tall and slender; showing her domination and command. The shoes would have to be brown, although brown wasn't a natural complement for red, brown shoes would suggest she was friendly, yet serious and down to earth. Charlotte felt a shiver of ecstasy as she enjoyed the vision she painted in front of her, goose pimples covered her arms and gave her the look of a plucked turkey, she was on a high and that high lasted as she journeyed to school, even until 10:45, when she got the news.

George had been let go.

He had been asked to leave by the governors. Contract terminated. Charlotte was crestfallen. All that work, all that effort, all the planning, all the forward-thinking, all the investment. Her head was swirling, and she needed to lie down or at least sit before she fainted. George was gone or at least going. All her work had come to nought; she had done everything to align herself with that man, now he was going! Who would take over and how quickly would she be able to build a new relationship? To inhale the putrid smell of the toilets just to wait for him —to have those one-minute conversations-all for nothing. He was privy to the secret recordings! All for nothing.

Charlotte made her way to the year nine office and was glad to find it empty. She cried, no bawled, allowing snot to form and freely run; it was a while before she came to.

Being resilient, Charlotte knew there was always a way forward she just couldn't figure out yet how she would proceed. She had to focus now on getting herself ready for the class she had in 20 minutes and ensure there were no traces of her little meltdown; things would seem clearer or at least more hopeful tomorrow. In fact, the worst that could come out of it was a good reference. Charlotte took her cleansing wipes from her handbag just as her mobile began to ring. She wasn't in much of a chatting mood but still glanced at the screen to see the caller, it was her mum. And at 11:15 Charlotte received even more devastating news.

Her Gran had died.

This time she crumbled, she folded like a deck chair, and tears afresh found her face. There was no one to Charlotte like her Gran. She sobbed uncontrollably, way past the time for her lesson and that was how Sean found her.

He embraced her in his arms and rocked her gently. Always asking what the matter was and stating he never thought he would see her cry. She just shook and couldn't find the words; she only had enough left in her to gesture to her phone. He released her just long enough to call the office to briefly explain there was an emergency and that her class needed to be covered. He went back to holding her tight.

They remained that way for as long as was decent.

Chapter 23

The sewage tank has burst, and raw sewage has been running again in areas of the school. Each time the problem had been fixed there was a new leakage. The school was infected and contaminated to the core. Diseases were prevalent and the army that had fought so bravely, through so many wars, was now dying. Many suffered from battle fatigue. A few had been executed for cowardice, some had been discharged, considered unsuitable for the military. There were three suicides. There were more and more diagnoses of Trench foot and Post Traumatic Stress Disorder every week. Families had fallen apart; there were thoughts to create a war nursery for the children who were victims of war and abandoned children were to be given over to foster care. Long-time lovers were now distant memories and there were only a few doctors in the house to administer care or offer solutions. They themselves were ravaged: such were the effects of high explosive landmines.

The army kept on high alert so long didn't have a fight or flight response anymore, never mind cortisol was speeding up heart rates, digestion was slowing down, blood flow to major muscle groups was being cut off, other automatic nervous functions were changing. Chronic stress was causing damage to the body. The army was dying and realisation that something had to change was the only thing they had in common. So everyone awaited a time of peace, the end of the war and desired the disturbed calm that was sure to follow. Everyone waited for Monday when they would see the first results of peace talks and the army would know if it was time to start the clean-up and the rebuild.

Chapter 24

The grey clouds have gathered, and the clouds are puffy (obvious pathetic fallacy but let's work with it). They are about to burst with rain, but the sun is defiant, not giving up that easy. Between each initial light drizzle there is a burst of sunshine.

It is Monday and there is a momentous meeting in the hall, the staffroom was just not conducive. The staff had been placed into teams. They were starting with an intradepartmental teambuilding and relaxation exercise. Groupings were a mix and match of departments and as you entered the hall, you checked on the mounted list to see the table you should join. The groupings are usually unlucky, you sit with a bunch of people you had never spoken to before and hope never to speak to again and after staring with boredom at each other someone involuntarily assumes group leadership until the others awaken.

While the sorting and settling down takes place several important people take their seats to the front of the hall, three of them are unfamiliar. The chair of governors is there with his usual tight-arsed self and the woman beside him was involved in education in the borough-most people forgot what she did.

In three minutes, a throat is cleared, and the meeting is called to order. The chair of governors moves towards the makeshift podium and begins to address the staff. He doesn't get very far before a mobile phone rings and everyone turns to see who the retard is. She quickly rummages through her handbag and switches it off. The chair uses this opportunity to ask anyone else with a mobile to switch if off or put it on silent. He continues with his speech, the all too familiar ramblings about the difficult time the school had recently endured and how the borough was in full support of its improvement and was doing all it could to help and so on and so forth. Staff by now was used to sleeping with their eyes wide open as he carried on. But that soon changed-Everyone became alert as he introduced the very short man wearing the brown suit with the yellow tie. He looked like a rejected conservative.

The chair of governors had just introduced the new headteacher.

He walked spritely to the podium, smiled and started to speak; his voice had surprising command. Expressions like: action plan, improvement, lesson planning, new appointments, accountability, restructuring, monitoring, discipline, overstaff, redundancies, were spewing like water from a broken pipe all over the teachers, and he continued to speak with conviction. Every teacher listened intently, and everyone took what they wanted to from his speech, and every single teacher began to decide where they would fit into his new plans and created a vision of their future. There was no doubt it was a time of change; now they knew the result of peace talk.

Mary, Sean and Charlotte had found themselves at the same table for the team-building exercise and they too like the rest of the staff were dazed. Nobody spoke, even though they could. The silence sat and invaded the space for a moment. A book fell from the top of the old piano in the corner and shattered the quiet; it was only then that tongues reminded themselves that they could speak. It was Sean who leant forward in an almost conspiratorial tone and said

'What did you make of that then?'

They were again silent for a while; and then Mary broke.

'I want out!'

'Where would you teach? Where would you prefer to go? 'he queried.

'You don't understand. I want out. Out of this profession, out of teaching, out of this poor imitation of a life!'

Charlotte listened intently. She said nothing. But Mary was now unstoppable.

'I quit! I absolutely quit! I have had enough of the politics, the overload of paperwork, the stressful observation process, the hours, the marking, and the lack of promotion!'

She paused for breath and continued.

'The administration, the unruly pupils, the impossible demands to get pupils who can't even read impressive exam results! The parents who insult you even when you are giving blood for their children.'

Mary wasn't finished.

'The low pay in comparison to other professions, the bullying from managers who were themselves being bullied to accomplish the impossible, creativity sacrificed in favour of exam driven teaching.'

'And OFSTED, DAMN OFSTED!'

Mary visibly exhaled and inhaled but couldn't stop.

'The immoral judgements schools make because of money-decisions that harmed children, and work-life-balance what the hell is that? Incompetent colleagues who tell you, you're incompetent! "The loss of self-confidence-the corruption of the soul!'

Sean interjected telling Mary she was speaking too loudly and others were looking at them.

'I don't care.' She belted back. 'I want out!'

Charlotte listened to Mary and identified with a little of what she said. She would never admit that she had had similar thoughts in a low moment when George had left and her gran had died. She had really wondered if being a teacher was worth it, she had thought about what life would be like if she gave it up but had quickly brushed the thought aside. She had already invested too much and had painted her linear vision straight to the top of the game. To give up now was just unfathomable.

She still didn't break her silence.

'I'm hanging around for a little while longer. Charlotte do you remember the deputy head of year job I spoke to you some time ago about? The interviews were yesterday; I think I got it-the extra dosh could do me good since I'm thinking of settling down soon.' He coloured, thinking about what a man of his background and heritage could achieve.

Charlotte was startled but tried her best not to show it, she only smiled. Sean continued.

'Mary, I think when you get home later and have a cuppa you'll reconsider, don't be discouraged, as they say, can you light a fire? Those who can, teach.'

Mary didn't answer her only response was to dip her hand in her handbag and rummage around, then peering in; intently she looked for something and found it. Mary produced a full box of matches and with no hint of amusement took one look at her surroundings and responded.

'Let it burn.'

Sean chuckled refusing to entertain the implications of Mary's actions, but Charlotte was distracted. She had seen the little man in the brown suit and yellow tie leave the hall, she saw the direction in which he headed, and she knew what she had to do.

Charlotte excused herself and vowed to hover by the toilets.

Final Chapter

And me, as for me, the simple class teacher with a love of teaching? The first-person narrator hiding behind the third. I crouch behind my broken classroom door wielding my metaphorical machete, guarding territory as I never thought I would, mentally beheading anyone who dares to deem my lesson unsatisfactory or my practice ineffective. I am shrinking into gangland the only place where it is safe.

Me, I'm a self-confessed gangster, dreaming of the riot, the rebellion, the jihad against red tape, unnecessary accountability, pointless change, fixed lesson structures, and the renaming of what already exists.

I want a gang, alumni gangsters who will gather brambles, matches, fuel-anything that will spark. After all, "Those who can teach, light a fire" or better yet, "What do teachers make?" A revolution. That's what.

Blurb

Think you know about teaching? Think again. It's the most rewarding and entertaining profession on the planet.

Inside you will find issues any professional, in any field can relate to, and of course, you'll meet some characters that I am sure you already know.

Teaching is an adventure and teachers are a special breed.

The cry of the proletariat?

No, Not really.

Read, relax and laugh.

Printed in the United States
By Bookmasters